The
Drop of Doom

Kids Can Read ® Kids Can Read is a registered trademark of Kids Can Press Ltd.

Text © 2002 Adrienne Mason
Illustrations © 2002 Pat Cupples
Revised edition © 2007

Kids Can Press acknowledges the financial support of the Government of Ontario, through the Ontario Media Development Corporation's Ontario Book Initiative; the Ontario Arts Council; the Canada Council for the Arts; and the Government of Canada, through the BPIDP, for our publishing activity.

Published in Canada by
Kids Can Press Ltd.
29 Birch Avenue
Toronto, ON M4V 1E2

Published in the U.S. by
Kids Can Press Ltd.
2250 Military Road
Tonawanda, NY 14150

www.kidscanpress.com

Adapted by David MacDonald and Adrienne Mason from the book *The Carnival Caper*.

Edited by David MacDonald
Designed by Kathleen Collett

Printed and bound in Singapore

The hardcover edition of this book is smyth sewn casebound.
The paperback edition of this book is limp sewn with a drawn-on cover.

CM 07 0 9 8 7 6 5 4 3 2 1
CM PA 07 0 9 8 7 6 5 4 3 2 1

Library and Archives Canada Cataloguing in Publication

Mason, Adrienne
    The drop of doom / written by Adrienne Mason ; illustrated by Pat Cupples.

(Kids Can read)
Previously published as: The carnival caper, 2002.
ISBN-13: 978-1-55453-035-9 (bound) ISBN-10: 1-55453-035-0 (bound)
ISBN-13: 978-1-55453-036-6 (pbk.) ISBN-10: 1-55453-036-9 (pbk.)

I. Cupples, Patricia II. Title. III. Series: Kids Can read (Toronto, Ont.)

GV1548.D526 2007   jC813'.54   C2006-903852-X

Kids Can Press is a *Corus*™ Entertainment company

The
Drop of Doom

Written by Adrienne Mason

Illustrated by Pat Cupples

Kids Can Press

Clancy watched some ants march by.

He scratched his belly.

He sniffed at a fly.

He sighed.

Clancy missed Lu.

Would she ever come home?

Lu and Clancy were best friends.

They were dog detectives, too.

They found lost puppies,

and stolen pies,

and missing shoes,

and sometimes more.

Clancy rolled onto his back

and yawned.

Then he heard a giggle.

Suddenly, something jumped

on top of him.

Lu was home!

"I am going to the carnival

with my cousin Jake," said Lu.

"Come with us."

Clancy shook his head.

He did not like Jake

or the magic tricks Jake did.

One time, Jake turned

Clancy's piggy bank into a rock.

He never changed it back.

"We can have cotton candy

and hot dogs," said Lu.

Clancy shook his head.

"We can ride the Drop of Doom," said Lu.

Clancy's ears perked up!

Lu and Clancy loved the Drop of Doom.

It was the best ride at the carnival.

It was the scariest, too!

Lu and Clancy got their bikes.

"Drop of Doom, here we come!"

said Clancy.

"First we need to get Jake,"

said Lu.

Lu and Clancy raced to the carnival.

Jake could hardly keep up.

"Look, the Drop of Doom!" said Lu.

"Let's go for a ride!" said Clancy.

"The D-d-d-drop of Doom?" said Jake.

Jake did not like rides.

He *really* did not like the Drop of Doom.

Lu and Clancy were ready to ride

the Drop of Doom.

But where was Jake?

"Oh no," said Lu.

"Jake is going to the magic tent."

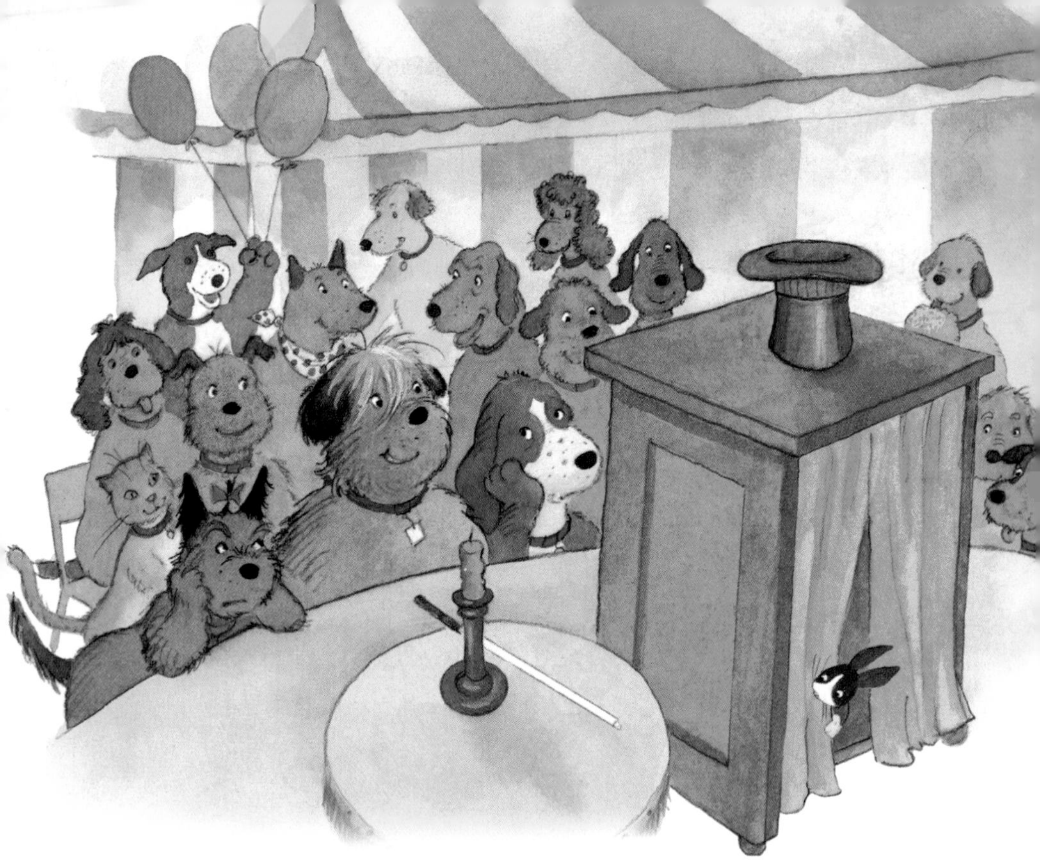

Lu and Clancy followed Jake

into the magic tent.

"I love magic tricks," said Jake.

But Lu wanted to ride the Drop of Doom.

"Maybe Clancy has a plan to get us

out of here," thought Lu.

Lu turned to Clancy.

Clancy had his ear against the tent wall.

"What does he hear?" wondered Lu.

Clancy heard a mean voice.

He heard someone say, "Drop of Doom"

and then he heard a big burp.

The voices kept talking.

Clancy stuck his head outside the tent

to hear better.

"Horace, stop eating and listen,"

someone said.

"Okay, Frank," said Horace.

"Here is the plan," said Frank.

Horace burped.

"We will make the Drop of Doom stop

when everyone is upside down," said Frank.

"Their purses and money

will fall to the ground.

Then we steal everything. Got it?"

Horace burped.

Clancy told Lu about

Horace and Frank's plan.

"We need to stop them!" said Lu.

"We have to get help," said Clancy.

"We need to get to the Drop of Doom,"

said Lu.

Lu and Clancy burst out of the magic tent.

They ran right into a hot dog cart.

"Watch it, kids!" said a dog

with a mean voice.

The other dog burped.

A mean voice and a burp?

It had to be Horace and Frank!

"Let's follow them!" said Clancy.

Just then, Jake found Lu and Clancy.

"Jake, we have to go!" cried Lu.

"We have to get to the Drop of Doom."

"Not so fast," said Jake.

"First we go to the Hall of Mirrors."

Hall
of
Mirrors

Jake had fun in the Hall of Mirrors.

Lu and Clancy did not.

They needed to get to the Drop of Doom.

But Jake had other ideas.

He wanted to take a dancing lesson.

Next, Jake made Lu and Clancy go

to the House of Horrors.

After that, he took them to the Pirate Hall.

It seemed like Jake would do *anything*

to stay away from the Drop of Doom.

It was getting late.

Lu and Clancy needed to stop

Horace and Frank.

"Lu, how can we get Jake to go

to the Drop of Doom?" whispered Clancy.

Lu had an idea.

Lu borrowed a card and

a pair of scissors.

She waved the card at Jake.

"Can you find a way to walk

through this card?" said Lu.

"If you can do it, we will not ride

the Drop of Doom," said Clancy.

Jake stared at the card.

He clipped a small hole,

but he could only get his big toe through.

He made the hole bigger.

He could only get

his nose through.

"I give up," Jake sighed.

Lu grabbed another card.

She cut here and snipped there.

In a flash, she *and* Clancy

walked through the card!

"Let's go!" cried Clancy.

"To the Drop of Doom!" yelled Lu.

Jake grabbed his tummy

and groaned.

Lu and Clancy made a plan.

"You find Horace, and I will find Frank,"

said Lu.

They sent Jake to get help.

Lu climbed on the Drop of Doom.

Clancy grabbed a banana.

A banana?

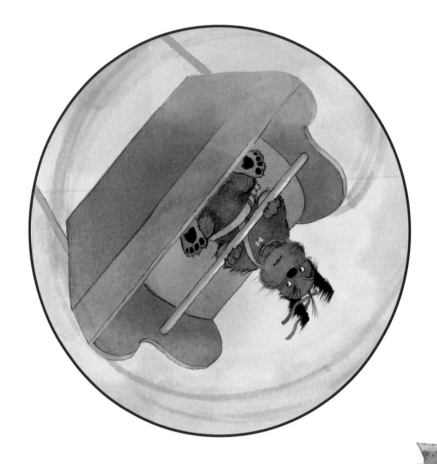

Lu sat in a car on the Drop of Doom.

The wind blew through her fur.

Suddenly the ride stopped.

Money and purses and watches

fell to the ground.

Down on the ground, Frank shouted,

"Grab the loot, Horace!"

But Horace did not move.

He was watching the banana

in Clancy's hand.

Lu saw Frank stealing the loot.

"I have to do something," thought Lu.

She climbed from car to car.

She borrowed belts and scarves

and necklaces.

Then she tied them together.

Lu swung down from the Drop of Doom.

POW!

She landed right on top of Frank.

Jake came back with Detective Doberman

and his police van.

"I will look after this crook,"

said Detective Doberman.

Clancy dropped pieces of banana.

Horace ate up each piece.

Clancy threw the banana into the police van.

Horace jumped in after it.

Detective Doberman shut the doors.

The crowd cheered!

"You did a fine job of stopping those

crooks," said Detective Doberman.

"Let's ride the Drop of Doom!" said Clancy.

"Yippee," yelped Lu.

Jake just groaned.

Lu's Amazing Card Trick

Ask an adult to help you do Lu's amazing card trick (see page 24). You will need a piece of regular size paper (like computer paper) and scissors.

1. Fold the paper in half, as shown. Cut a piece out of the folded edge to make it look like the picture.

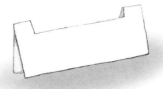

2. Cut the paper along the lines shown below. Never cut right through to the other edge. Make 13 cuts.

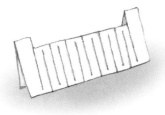

3. Carefully unfold the paper and pull it open to make a big circle. Now you can walk right through!